Nancy Smith born in the 60s, grew up in the 70s, has always read mystical and thrillers. When not working, she is either reading or writing her own. You will find her on weekends travelling around for new ideas either in a camper van or riding pillion on a motorbike, always with a pen and notepad with her. She lives in a village east of York with her husband.

To my mum, Barbara and Les for reading everything, I wrote and for believing in me.

Nancy Smith

NANCY'S MAGIC

A Collection of Magic,
Mystery, Suspense and
Travel Stories

AUSTIN MACAULEY PUBLISHERS™

LONDON • CAMBRIDGE • NEW YORK • SHARJAH

A CIP catalogue record for this title is available from the British Library.

ISBN 9781398420625 (Paperback)
ISBN 9781398420632 (ePub e-book)

www.austinmacauley.com

First Published 2022
Austin Macauley Publishers Ltd®
1 Canada Square
Canary Wharf
London
E14 5AA

I acknowledge Austin Macauley publishers for giving me the chance.

Table Of Contents

Pendle Child

The little girl ran up and down the street. Her pointy hat, held on by elastic, kept slipping to one side; her black cape, dotted with stars, flowing behind her.

"I'm going to be a witch!" she cried out to one of the neighbours. "When I grow up, I'm going to be a witch."

"That's nice, dear," the woman smiled at the lively six-year-old girl, long hair in natural curls, eyes shining bright.

Her mother sighed, ever since they had taken Louise on a trip to see the supposed local witch's cave.

According to the local folklore, she had made herbs and potions to heal others, including animals.

Twenty years later, the mother sat at the dining table and sighed again. Her fingers nervously picking the lace on the tablecloth. Louise, her daughter, had never grown out of the idea of wanting to be a witch. She now grew herbs and sold them in her little shop, with other natural healing ointments. Strange, how she often knew things or saw shadows of people or animals who were long gone.

May be it was time to tell her the truth, if only James was here. But her husband was gone now, nearly two years since he had passed away.

Louise entered the dining room and sat opposite her mother, noticing all the newspaper cuttings. The headlines screaming at her:

Baby found on Pendle Hill!
Girl found abandoned on Pendle Hill in a crib made of heather!
Witch baby found!

Louise read them all and looked questioningly at her mother.

"Time to tell you the truth, Louise, about where you came from," replied her mother.

"Dad and I found you on Pendle Hill whilst we were out walking. No one came forward to the appeals in the press. Possibly a young woman left you there, hoping someone else would be able to take better care of you than she could." Trying to keep her voice steady, her mother carried on, "We moved away to here where no one knew of us and the story, and a few months later, we legally adopted you. As far as we were concerned, you were and still are our daughter. And I am so proud of you, your dad was too."

The young woman's eyes opened wider in amazement. "I knew I was different, I never seemed to fit in anywhere. Friends thought I was a freak if I called to animals and they came for a pat."

Her mother reached over and held her hand. "I was so worried in case there was a knock on the door and someone came to claim you. But look at you now, all grown up, a little shop and herb garden."

"I always wondered how I knew things, what herbs to use and how much was needed. I couldn't understand when I could see animals following people down the street or dogs sat outside a shop waiting, but no one else could see them." Louise got up and gave her mother a hug. "I couldn't have asked for better parents. I will see you tomorrow as usual for tea."

Walking the short distance back to her little flat over the shop, a voice called out, "Louiseianna!"

Ignoring the voice, she stepped into a little side street café, sitting down, lost in her thoughts, becoming aware that she had company at her table, a young woman sat opposite her "Louiseianna," the stranger whispered.

"I'm sorry but my name is Louise. I think you have mistaken me for someone else." She noticed the woman's long wavy hair, so similar to her own, her clothes well-worn but not tatty.

The stranger whispered again, "Louiseianna of Pendle Hill. Do not be afraid of me. You were the child of a witch who fell in love with a townie. But we knew we could not keep you. How could he explain to his parents, witches are not meant to exist? And would have been in even more trouble as it is forbidden, we are supposed to keep to our own."

Louise listened, dumbstruck.

The woman carried on, "He left the country and I needed to return to my own family. I saw a young couple walking over the moors. I made a split-second decision. You have done well, my child. I have watched you grow and will carry on but from afar." The woman stood up. "Now I must go, but first, my name is Rowanna of Pendle. Here." She passed over a piece of paper. Louise sat, trying to take it all in, as the

13

woman, with a smile on her face and with a few clicks of her fingers, vanished.

I'm losing my mind, Louise thought, till she noticed the piece of paper. Carefully unfolding it to find a short message.

"Louiseianna of Pendle, grow strong, use your talents for the good. And never forget to sing and dance in the rain."

Leaving the café, her puzzled look turned to a smile and then laughter as the rain started to slowly fall. And she did what she had always done ever since she was a little girl, dance in the rain…

All That Glitters

Clutching the bag tightly to her, she ran towards her car. Throwing the bag onto the passenger seat, making sure it was secure, she fastened her seat belt and started the engine. She loved the sound her engine made. She never noticed the curtain move. Her hands clutched the steering wheel, then indicated to pull out. She thought to herself, *No other traffic, good.*

Alice wondered how long it would be before it was noticed that she wasn't there and most of all, neither were the stones. The thought made her smile. Diamonds, emeralds, rubies, sapphires, all glistening rocks and now they were hers. Taking one hand off the wheel, she thumped the air in triumph.

The excitement had made her thirsty, she slapped the steering wheel as she drove. "Stupid," she muttered to herself. "Nothing to drink."

Pulling onto the side, she re-watched over and scrambled in her little bag. Her fingers brushed against the stones. Grinning, she pulled out a small bag of sweets. "Hmph, jelly babies. Too old for these but they will do."

Her heart was heating quickly as she thought about them waking up and finding that she and the stones had gone.

Hitting the pedal, she carried on driving, too late to go back now, humming quietly to herself, she tried not to think what would happen if they caught her. The stones must be worth an awful lot of money, hundreds, maybe thousands. She could get a new car with an open top. Her friends would be so jealous, especially Lucy, she was always coming over to show off a new dress or coat; this would show her.

Stopping the car, she looked out of the windows, the coast was clear, no-one was following her.

The urge to run her fingers through the stones was strong. Lifting the bag onto her lap, she looked inside. Putting her hand in, she let the stones fall through her fingers, cool to the touch.

Alice knew she was in trouble. However, she had not been able to resist them, sitting there in a bowl, shining at her, daring her to take them. Many times, she had reached out for them but had always been stopped.

Not thinking of what would happen, she had got up early and put her plan into action. Knowing that she must keep driving, her life depended on it.

Listening, no sirens! *Good, they would not call the police, they couldn't.*

Using one hand to shield her eyes from the glare of the morning sun, her other hand on the wheel, she muttered, "Where are my sunglasses?"

There they were on the other seat, swerving as she reached and slipped them on, Alice spoke out, "Back to some driving, many miles to do, girl."

So focused on her driving and where she was going, she jumped when a large shadow appeared at the side of the car.

"Oh boy, am I in trouble now?"

She screeched to a halt as her door was flung open.

"Alice May Young, get in the house. I'm surprised you're not dizzy driving round and round the garden."

The six-year curly-haired girl plucked off her bright pink plastic sunglasses and grinned at her mum.

"I was just playing, Mum."

Trying not to laugh at her daughter, the young mother carried on, "Yes, and it's time for dinner; and can I have the coloured glass stones back in the vase please?"

8 Knights

Pacing up and down the living room floor, the man spoke, "You have to listen to me, to understand. There are 8 knights, they don't know it but times will change and everything as we know will change."

Laura didn't know what to say, she was transfixed. It seemed so much like a fantasy world he was telling her about. But deep down, she knew that he spoke the truth.

He took a deep breath before carrying on, "When the time comes, they will, by instinct, come together and work together. Just as they have always done and always will. Like their fathers and grandfathers and before."

Taking a sip of the tea Laura had made him, then taking a pull on the e-cigarette, he spoke, "God, I hate these things but it's the closest hit I can get from being a twenty-a-day man."

Laura looked around the room. She and Luke, her boyfriend, had made the flat as homely as possible. He only worked for a couple of hours on a Saturday morning, so would be back shortly.

Next, she studied the man, he was a friend of Luke's but from the minute she met him, she knew that she could trust him and had no qualms about letting him in to wait for Luke. She tuned back into what he was saying.

"Some will be friends, others will be strangers, but they will greet each other like long lost friends."

"But when? Why?" she stammered.

He looked at her, studied her as he sipped his tea. Could she really do what he was going to ask? The young woman hadn't mocked him but had listened, drinking it all in, asking the occasional question.

He had only met her a few times but he knew of her, of being in touch with what others could not see. She was the one, the one person who could keep the knights together, of that, he had been told. Those dark nights when he had been sat, talking and listening near the old mausoleum in the cemetery. Knowledge was passed on.

The middle-aged biker reached over and took her hand.

"You and they will know what to do when the time is right. It is in your blood. Survival is in your soul. Your job is to keep them together until the job is done. When that happens, they will split up, go their separate ways but will always unite when needed." He stood up to stretch his legs "To believe and not to lose heart, that is the key."

Sitting back down, he leant forward. "Luke told me you were having bad dreams, dreams what made you scared to go to bed. Sometimes he found you on the floor by the door, leaning against it, asleep holding the handle. He has also heard knocks on the door and the light shining under the door going dark, as if someone is stood there. I would like you to draw me what you are seeing."

Laura found a pen and a piece of paper, and did a rough sketch, before passing it to him. He tried not to let his face change. *Hell and damnation*, he thought before standing up and heading for the door, turning to look at her. "I need to go and see someone about this. I will be back shortly."

Laura just sat there, her thoughts all over the place, she needed to focus. There was only one thing which always used to calm her down, her rune stone bag. Many times she would sit there, hand in the bag of stones, moving them between her fingers. They settled her.

An hour had nearly passed before she opened the door to him again.

He stood there, looking at her, before sitting down.

"I went to see someone, as you will know about all of this and we have both come to the same conclusion." He held up the drawing. "This is bad, it does not get any worse than this. My friend went to see the person who sent you this and it is as I thought. He is scared of you. Does not know you but knows of you, especially with what he dabbles in." Taking a deep breath, he carried on, "You have to face it, tell it you are not scared of it anymore. Once you do that, your nights should be dreamless. Now I need to go and rest my weary bones, and clear mv head." He turned around at the door to face Laura for the final time. "Remember, the key is to believe and to keep heart. Tell Luke I will see him later."

That night, Laura laid in the bed, Luke snoring gently at her side. It was now or never.

"OK, whatever you are, I am not scared of you anymore. Come and face me."

Laying there, not knowing what was going to happen, if anything. She felt a hand touch her feet, then her arm. Next, it moved around her head and face. She kept muttering, "Go. I am not scared of you anymore." A cold wind swept around the room and then nothing. In her dreams that night, its face appeared once more but it was blotted out by an old man in a long flowing robe, holding a staff in one hand and the other hand on a planet. All at once, she felt at peace.

Weeks passed, she heard from Luke that his friend had died. Stomach cancer, it seemed. Sometimes she thought she could see him in the shadows or hear him. Maybe it was her imagination.

She rarely thought of the conversation about the knights, kept it quiet from Luke. But maybe his friend had told him, as she would often catch him staring at her.

Then one day, taking his leathers off after being on a motorbike ride with three of his friends, he said, "Hope you don't mind, Laura, but I will be going out for a short ride out tonight. Meeting up with the other three and they have invited some of their friends. I said it would be okay if we came back for coffee and sit in the garden. There will be about eight of us…"

The Wizard's Stone

Lucy edged nearer to the stone, daring herself to touch it.

Nonsense! Really! I mean it's just a stone, she thought to herself.

The locals were full of stories and having grown up in the village, she had heard them all years ago.

Nervously, she looked around, even as a child she had kept away from here. But now at nineteen, she felt grown up enough to touch it. Maybe just to prove that it was nothing magical and it was just as it looked, a large stone.

The locals had even put a little wooden fence around the bottom of it but why, she had no idea. Her hand reaching out, then flat against the top of it. Before lifting it back off, scrutinising her hand and every finger. Nothing amiss; looking around her, nothing. Feeling foolish, she laughed; still giggling to herself as she made her way home.

Her mum was busy in the kitchen. "Hi, Mum, remind me the story of the stone please."

Her mother turned around from the stove. "Well, Lucy, it's just a stone, a tall stone, which the locals named The Wizard's Stone. It goes that he used to cast his magic on the top of it but he fell in love with a local girl. Her father came whilst they were walking hand in hand and dragged her away." Lucy's mother turned back to turn a pan off, before carrying on, "The wizard swore that he would wait for her, all nonsense really. Just a fairy tale."

That night, Lucy slept badly, tossing and turning. She woke up totally drained, thank goodness it was the weekend and she did not have to go to work.

The birds were singing and the sun was shining. She glanced at the clock, nearly eight o'clock. Too restless to try and go back to sleep, she made her way downstairs. Grabbing her coat and bag, she beaded out.

Somehow she found herself heading towards the stone. Lucy gasped as she noticed a small posy of wildflowers laid on top of it. The flowers were small and pretty, tied together with a satin ribbon. Looking around and seeing no one, she reached for them, but pulled her hand back at the last minute. As beautiful as they were, they could have been left for someone else.

With a deep sigh, she turned to go back home but stopped, hearing footsteps behind her. A young man of about twenty with black shoulder length hair and piercing blue eyes stood by the stone, holding the posy, smiling at her.

"They are for you. I saw you yesterday by the stone. A pretty lady should have pretty flowers." He bowed, holding the posy out to her.

Hesitantly, she took them. "They are lovely, thank you; but why me?"

He shrugged his shoulders. "It was to see you smile."

Lucy wondered if he had just moved to the area, not having seen him before. "Do you live 'round here?"

The young man flung his arm out in a direction. "Yes, not far from here. But why? What draws you to the stone?"

Lucy looked at it. "The locals say it belonged to a wizard." She laughed nervously, thinking that he would find her immature. "I mean wizards don't exist, they are fairy tales, but it is such a sad tale of two people who could not be together."

She stopped as she noticed his expression change, he looked so sad that she reached out and touched his arm. Flinching, he took a step back, before noticing the look of alarm that crossed her face.

"Sorry, Lucy, just memories. Now I must go." The young man turned and began to walk away.

"Wait!" she cried out. "Will I see you again?"

Stopping, he turned to look back at her and gave her a little bow. "Maybe, who knows?"

Setting off back the way she had come, she suddenly came to a halt, hand on her forehead as realisation hit.

She muttered to herself, "My name, he knew my name."

Looking back, she half-hoped that he was still there, but no, he had gone. That night, the dreams were so vivid, walking through fields, hand in hand, laughing, dancing, her long dress flowing out as she twirled around. Then tears and screams as she was dragged away, shouting out to him. Pleading with him to save her, to wait for her.

Slipping out of the house early next morning, she tried to make sense of the dream, heading towards the stone, hoping he was there.

Her heart beating faster as he stood there, holding out his hand. Her fingers entwined with his. Lucy had a feeling of belonging, it felt so right. Somehow she knew that no matter what he asked, she would go with him.

"Lucy?" her mother called, knocking on her closed bedroom door. Hearing no reply, she stepped in, not noticing a posy of wilted flowers on the windowsill.

In the kitchen, she turned to face her husband, heart heavy but not knowing why.

"Gone off on one of her walks. Never mind. I'll tell her when she comes back about the stone collapsing and scattered all over the ground…"

The Survivor

Inside everyone, no matter how deep in us, is the primal instinct to survive, no matter what.

Waking up to a glorious sunny day, the sky was blue, not a cloud in sight, I had an uneasy feeling in the pit of my stomach. Something was wrong, really wrong; but what?

After washing and dressing, could not face any breakfast, turning on the radio for the morning show.

Nothing but static on all stations. OK, so maybe the batteries were dead, so tried the television, nothing! This was really weird.

By now, I was feeling a little bit scared and reached for the phone. Typical, no signal!

Picking up my bag and deciding a trip to the shops about a quarter of a mile away would help dispel the feeling.

It was too quiet, no birds singing, no children laughing, no-one about. No dogs roaming, no cats slouching on the walls.

By this time, I was running, heading to the bridge which crossed the river, the only way to reach the main road and the small parade of shops.

Glancing down and stopping dead in my tracks, I looked again. Dead fish and other dead wildlife were floating in the river.

Hoping, praying, reaching the road, silently crying for a sign of life. Anyone!

No cars, no one at all, the shops were shut and most had their blinds down.

Running from door to door, frantic! Banging on the doors as I went past. Silence.

Climbing over a wall and tripping over a broken-down fence, reaching the back of the general store.

Knocking on the door and windows. Holding my breath, trying the door handle and swung the door open. Creeping in, not knowing what to expect.

This was weird, in the owner's little kitchen, the remains of a meal left on the table, a coat draped over a chair. Where in God's name was everyone?

Food, I needed to stock up, entering the store, filling my bag with tinned food, torch and batteries. Reaching home, racking my brain for an explanation, it was impossible. Searching the adjoining homes for anything to give me a clue. The house phones were dead, no pets, no sign of life. Taking the bicycle I found in a hallway, it would be easier to search the rest of the village.

Standing in the middle of the road, arms wide out, I shouted, "What the hell is going on?"

Back in my kitchen, I replaced the batteries and sat patiently, slowly turning the dial on the radio. Maybe, just maybe.

"...Now back to the emergency situation concerning the village of Wellditch. The government are still undecided as to

27

whether the village is safe or if it should be destroyed, following the explosion at a nearby chemical plant. One hundred people were instantly killed and many more people have been infected. All the roads have now been barricaded by at least seven feet of barbed wire and are being patrolled by the military. The latest report is that another fifty people have died from the effects, and fish and wildlife have been seen in the river. The environment agency is making plans to block the river in the affected section. Any remaining livestock have been removed to neighbouring farms. This concludes the special broadcast."

Switching off the radio, she sat down and started to sob.

"What about me?" she repeated over and over again.

Pouring stiff drink, trying to calm down and think back. Arriving home from a business meeting abroad. Exhausted after a six-hour flight, I had directed the taxi driver to take a back-country lane as it was quicker. Taken a couple of sleeping tablets and gone straight to bed.

No one had seen me arrive and no one would question where I was, having come back a day earlier than planned.

Reaching into a drawer and slamming the bottle of sleeping tablets at the side of me, and grabbing a bottle of spirits, but couldn't do it. Picked up the pills and stared at them. One part of me was saying, "Take them!" and the other part of me was screaming, "Live!"

Placing them back where they belonged, I realised that I had to fight to survive.

Not knowing if it would do any good, swallowing a couple of aspirins, in case whatever it was had affected me. Would I still be here when someone came or would I die and be forgotten? They had said it wasn't safe, what was going to happen to me?

The next morning saw me cycling alone, a bit wobbly, not having rode one for years. I had to see the barricade for myself. Would anyone be there? What would happen if they saw me? Filled with fear, yet spurred me on, would they help me? I rode right up to the wire, touching it so I would know that all this was real and not some nightmare that I could wake up from.

There were four men in white suits, their faces covered by masks, sitting outside a caravan. My mouth opened but no words came out. One of them saw me, pointed whilst telling the others. Three words could be heard quite clearly.

"Oh my God!"

Turning around, I pedalled furiously, like the devil was after me. The suits and the masks had badly frightened me. Pulling up outside the house, leaving the bike propped up against the wall, I dashed inside and only then did I try and get my breath back. What a fool I'd been.

The first sign of life in a couple of days and I had fled like a frightened rabbit.

During the night, I woke up in a sweat, feeling sick. Just making it to the bathroom, head pounding, legs feeling like jelly. Dragging myself back to the bed, too weak to pull the sheets over me. Falling into a feverish sleep. Tossing, turning, every so often, stomach cramps racking my body. I came around having no idea of what day it was or even if it was day or night. Holding on to the wall, I pulled my weary body into the kitchen and switched on the radio to hear.

"…We know that there is one person still in the village, a young woman. We should know who she is after extensive checking but we will keep her identity to ourselves. If you are listening, please do as we ask. Try to keep your strength up, don't let it lag.

"The symptoms are similar to those of flu, sweating, hot and cold flushes, but you also may experience severe stomach cramps and vomiting. Be at the road block at one this afternoon, we will leave you a box. You will have to inject yourself, every three hours for two days. For you to live, you must have these injections. The scientists will not be allowed into the village for at least another three days to run tests and assist you. We wish you good luck and may God bless you."

Eyes full of tears, I turned it off. I was so weak, I just wanted to die but somewhere I found an inner strength that made me realise how much I wanted to live. It was now twelve, I had to leave.

Somehow managing to get on the bike, only to fall off it. So I walked down the middle of the lane, swaying, sometimes falling to my knees, then dragging myself up again. Walking from one side to the other, laughing out loud. How funny it would be for a police car to stop me and do me for being drunk and disorderly. But there wouldn't be any police today, tomorrow or the day after.

Reaching the barrier, the four men were there, plus an extra six. "Pick up the box, please, miss, and inject yourself every three hours," spoke one of them.

"Take me with you, please, get me out of here." I sobbed.

Another stepped forward. "Sorry, miss, but we do not know how badly you are infected. The way we have just seen you walk and how you look, I'd say pretty bad. The injections will help. Please listen to the radio for advice."

Somehow I made it home. I don't really remember. Never in all of my 26 years had I ever injected myself. With trembling hands, I found a vein, pushed in the plunger of the needle till the air bubble came out, then stabbed it into my arm. Letting the contents flow into my bloodstream. I set the alarm for every 3 hours, in case I fell asleep. This went on for two days, injecting, going to sleep, only to jump up when the alarm went off. At the end, I was a bit stronger. I was managing to keep down some soup which was heated over a camping stove. Everything was still a struggle, just to go from one room to another. According to the radio, the scientists were coming to get me out at 12 noon tomorrow.

It was half past nine when I woke up, there was a funny smell in the air. Switching on the radio, I heard the frantic voice of the presenter.

"...Lady! Get out! GO! If you are still alive, get the hell out, get to the barricade, you have no more time left. There was a second explosion, they are going to burn the village at 10:30."

By now, he was shouting. I ran to the window, they were early, smoke seemed to be everywhere. Did they think I was dead?

I had to get out. I was still weak. I didn't know if I could make it.

Covering my face and body as best as I could, I opened the door, then staggered back as the force of the heat hit me. I tried to run at first but it was no good, so settled down to a slow trot. It was all I could manage. On both sides, buildings were on fire. Half blinded by the smoke, I kept on going, stumbling over debris.

Collapsing on my knees, waiting to die, either by chemicals or smoke. I had gone through sheer hell for what? To die by the roadside? No, thanks! I staggered, crawled along the road.

Voices! Strong arms wrapped themselves around me.

"Okay, miss, we've got you, take it easy now, it's alright."

Wiping the grime off my tear-stained face, I was carried to a waiting ambulance. Before I lost consciousness, I knew everything was going to be alright, I was alive…

It's Only Make-Believe

A beautiful sunny day, birds were singing as the young woman got out of her bed. Flinging open the doors of the wardrobe, wondering what to wear. What would be suitable, going through all the luxurious clothes, scattering them all over.

"Good morning, ma'am." As her personal assistant entered the room, trying not to notice all the disarray that she would have to hang and fold, once the main decision had been made. She couldn't really complain, she had her own little flat attached to the house, with everything she needed and much more. Years ago, they bad been to school together but lost touch, until she had answered the advert in the Times.

"Morning, Christine. Just toast for breakfast, I think. I have a lunch appointment with a film producer and my agent, and then I have to attend a dinner party with Steven. God, I hate publicity parties; they can be such a bore."

The actress knew her husband, Steve, hated them too but put up with it as he adored his wife.

"Yes, ma'am," replied Christine as she left the room.

Samantha Jardine wandered through her home, still marvelling at how quick it had all happened.

One minute, a nobody-heard-of actress, the next, a top movie star with fans who lined the pavements hoping for a glimpse of her, or if they were really lucky, a photo. A talent scout had been highly impressed with one of her performances and it had escalated from there, hit after hit.

Of course, she had had to change her name, you couldn't be a star with a name like Carol Fisher.

Fame and fortune had followed quickly after two major films and her earnings had bought her this great ten-roomed house, a chauffeur-driven car, holidays abroad whenever they could be fitted in. More money than enough to make sure her parents were cared for.

The lunch went better than Samantha had hoped, another contract signed for a movie and the book had been a best seller so she had been the obvious choice.

Steven escorted her to the party. She knew by the envious glances that she had chosen well. But she couldn't get used to the way other women called her 'darling'.

Her hostess came to greet her, "Darling, you look fantastic, red does seem to suit you."

Of course the press were there. "This way, please, Miss Jardine. Look this way, Miss Jardine."

Till a voice shouted at her, "Carol! Carol Fisher! You have been daydreaming again!"

Carol sat up with a start, glaring at her classmates who were laughing at her.

"This has got to stop, you will see me after school for extra homework," spoke her teacher.

"Yes, miss," replied Carol. She would get back to her dreams later…

Against the Clock

The young mother moved around the room quickly, opening cupboards and drawers, placing the contents into boxes and bags. There wasn't much, they didn't have much. Most of her husband's wage went on the rent and the bills, and what she earned from her part-time job paid for food and whatever the children needed or what she could get for them from the markets and charity shops. Only once or twice had she had to visit the food bank when they had been hit with a hefty bill, usually the council tax.

Smiling at the thought of her children. Bobby was six, going on sixteen, and Janie was eight and a little madam.

Going around the second floor flat, it had been cramped but it was home, or it had been their home till about six weeks ago. Gripping the doorframe as she remembered her husband, Steve, coming through the door, ashen-faced, as she read and re-read the letter before clinging to him, sobbing.

They had managed to keep it quiet from everyone, including the children. They felt that they couldn't handle the hundred or so questions that they would be asked.

Wiping away a tear which was running down her face, the shock of what had happened still so hard to take in.

The children were at school, so there were still a few hours to finish the packing. They had to leave; they had no other choice.

Today and the following couple of days had been booked off work. It was enjoyable working in the small café, and she appreciated the company and the banter with the customers.

There wasn't much left to pack, not that they had much anyway. The furniture was staying, as it belonged to the flat. Going into the children's small shared bedroom, picking up the few toys that they had. They never complained or asked for all the latest gadgets and toys. The clothes they had were worn but still smart and clean, most had come from the markets or charity shops. She had got quite handy with a needle and thread, patching holes in jeans.

The other small bedroom, hers and Steve's, sitting on the stripped mattress, most of all their belongings had gone, all packed in boxes. Opening her jewellery box, not much, just a few bits of costume jewellery. All she really had was her wedding ring, the one pair of earrings and her mother's pendant. Anything else of value had been sold long ago.

Wiping away another tear which threatened to fall with the back of her hand. As much as they had struggled, they had been happy, the four of them. What was their future going to be like, especially for the children, new different lives?

Steve would be home soon; he had arranged to finish work early. The word *home* stuck in her throat and she stifled another sob.

A couple of hours later and that was it, the flat was bare of their personal belongings. The door opened and Steve came in, hugging his wife to him. "It's going to be fine. Let's get these few boxes loaded. I've borrowed a van so we can pick up the kids as well."

Closing the door on their old life, not looking back, they headed off to pick up the children.

"Mummy! Daddy!" the children screamed with delight as they ran to them and clambered into the van. Noticing they were not going the usual road to home, the questions came.

"Where are we going? Why aren't we going home?"

Jane held her brother's hand as he looked at her fearfully.

"Be patient, we are nearly there," replied Steve, smiling at them.

Twenty minutes later, they pulled up outside a semi-detached house. Turning around to look at them, their dad spoke, his eyes shining, a grin on his face, "This is our new home, kids."

They shrieked with delight as they got out and ran around the garden, then inside the house.

"A garden! We've got a garden and a bedroom, each! Can we have a puppy? A rabbit? A goldfish?"

Hand in hand, the couple made their way into the living room, smiling as their gaze locked onto a frame hanging above the fireplace. Inside the frame, a copy of their winning lottery ticket…

Run!!!

Running, running, stopping to catch her breath. Taking deep breaths to try and slow down her fast-beating heart. Julie knew she had to keep going and going. To stop, she did not bear thinking about. She was afraid, very afraid, running for her life.

Listening, straining over the sound of her panting for other footsteps. Wait! Were those headlights? A sigh of relief as they went past the end of the alley.

Slipping into a doorway, the scared young woman checked her bag, which had been clutched tightly in her hand. The money was still there, wrapped tightly in bundles. Knowing it was wrong to take the five grand which had been lying there but she needed it. How else would she have been able to leave him and his dodgy deals, not forgetting the thugs who worked for him.

The bundles had been there on the table, left as he went out in the evening. Without even thinking about what could happen, grabbing her coat, bundling the cash into her bag, she fled. Her phone flashed, a voice message.

"Julie?" he growled. "If you know what is good for you, bring the cash back."

Beep! Another message, this time more gentle, more like the man she used to know.

"Darling, please come back, it doesn't matter about the money. Keep it."

Then a third, more menacing. "Bitch, thought you could outsmart me, did you? I will find you."

Tears sprang into her eyes as she furiously rubbed them away.

What had she done? He would kill her!

Ignoring the thoughts which tumbled though her head, she made to move and froze—voices! Shrinking back against a door, holding her breath. A sigh of relief escaped as two drunks, laughing, wobbled past.

Where could she go? She had no family and the thugs would check all the hotels. But she didn't even have a credit card to pay for a room. He had made sure of that, no bank account, neither, just gave her cash every week or when she needed it. She had thought that he was just looking after her and not controlling.

No one would miss her, no one would report not seeing her, there was only him. She knew how his moods could change, sweet, gentle, one minute; the next, ranting and raving, usually over a deal which had not gone according to plan. Meeting her in a bar, he had had wined and dined her. At eighteen, she thought she was grown up enough and had been flattered. Before long, she had moved in.

Biggest mistake she had ever made, she thought bitterly.

"Think," Julie muttered. What to do, no buses or trains for at least eight hours but he would be searching the stations first thing, unless they caught her first.

She couldn't stay here, curled up in a doorway. A plan began to form in her tired mind. The abandoned wrecked garages near the station, shelter. Maybe she could hide in there for the night, shuddering at the thought of rats which were probably lurking inside them.

The phone beeped, a text message, reading it before switching it off.

"Coming for you, on our way."

Making her way across the roads, hiding if any cars appeared, reaching the garages, standing out against the moonlight. Stumbling inside one, finding a broken armchair, sinking into it, trying not to think of what else was sharing the dark dank space with her.

Waking with a start, the young woman rubbed her eyes, then ran her fingers through her hair. Daylight. She could see a bus pulling into the bus station.

Fumbling with the change in her pocket, one foot on the step as she began to board the bus, a hand on her shoulder.

"Julie! Julie!" the voice came again. She awoke, bed clothes wrapped around her as her head cleared.

Her head pounding that afternoon, she had gone for a lie down.

He stood there smiling, looking down at her. "Bad dreams, huh? C'mon, sleepy head, I'm just nipping out." Kissing her lightly on her forehead, he left the room. Hearing the front door close, she got up.

Still rubbing sleep from her eyes, Julie went down the stairs and gasped. Lying there on the table were a few large bundles of notes…

One Sunny Day

The young pilot hugged his wife tightly. "I'll come back to you, Mary. You and Jamie, just you wait and see."

He moved away and bending down, looked into his three-year son's eyes. "Look after your mum for me, Son." Ruffling his hair, Billy turned back to his wife. "I'll write, Mary, as often as I can."

Tears streaming down her face, holding her son's hand tightly, the young woman watched her husband, so smart in his RAF uniform, go to the vehicle which was waiting for him.

It was the beginning of 1945, and the many battles in the air were fierce. Mary had no idea where Billy was. Any letters which arrived were read and re-read over and over again. They were lovingly placed in a small drawer, wrapped around by a satin ribbon. These few days of Billy's weekend leave had been wonderful. He had joined up as soon as he was eighteen. Two years later, laughing and smiling, obtaining a special licence, they had got married. Two witnesses came in off the street and they celebrated by having half of mild in the Jack Dory's public house. This blasted war, when would it end, so many lives lost.

Till the telegraph came...

The years had been kind to Mary and Jamie, they had managed as best as they could. Mary had always made sure that they were both smart, becoming handy with a needle and thread. Through this, she had met Robert, the brother of a customer. He had treated Jamie like his own son.

Many happy years were spent with bucket and spades, football matches, ice cream and sausage rolls. As Jamie got older, he brought his girlfriends home. He had never forgotten his real dad, he had a photo of him in his room.

Robert and Mary spent forty happy years together but Robert was not a well man. He had survived Dunkirk but he had developed a lung infection, probably caused by the oil and diesel in the sea.

It had been held at bay over the years but now he was fighting a losing battle. Taking a turn for the worse, Robert passed away.

Mary sat gazing out of the window, she couldn't complain, two men who had loved her. On the table, lay Billy's letters, a tear ran down her face.

Jamie took his mother to the cemetery, she was now in her early seventies but every week, she visited the memorial to Billy, Jamie's dad.

Mary sat down on one of the benches. "Oh, Billy, I've missed you so much. I never stopped loving you."

"And I never stopped loving you," came the reply.

Jamie stood still, unable to move, remembering to breathe, as a young man in RAF uniform moved silently towards his mother, holding out his hand.

"I always said I would come back to you—its time."

Jamie watched open-mouthed as he saw his mother place her hand in pilot's, stood up and began to move away. They stopped and turned around. A salute from the pilot and a young woman blowing him a kiss. Then gone!

Jamie ran to where his mother sat. "Mum, did you see? Did you see him?" Then stopped. His mother's eyes closed, a smile on her face. He knew his dad had come back for her...